Bruno trusts Karen. He follows her every
lead, hangs on her every word.

Nothing scares her. Nothing intimidates
her. Nothing overwhelms her.

Right now, there's a dead body in the trunk of their
car—and despite Karen's laidback attitude, Bruno
feels scared, intimidated, and overwhelmed.

Should he still follow Karen?

R.W. WALLACE

Author of the Ghost Detective Series

SITTING DUCK

A CHILLING SHORT STORY

Sitting Duck

by R.W. Wallace

Copyright © 2019 by R.W. Wallace

Copy editing by Jinxie Gervasio
Cover by the author
Cover Illustration 18932336 © sergeyp | 123rf.com

All characters and events in this book, other than those clearly in the public domain, are fictitious and any resemblance to real persons, living or dead, is purely coincidental.

All rights reserved. No part of this publication may be reproduced, distributed, or transmitted in any form or by any means, including photocopying, recording, or other electronic or mechanical methods, without the prior written permission of the publisher, except in the case of brief quotations embodied in critical reviews and certain other noncommercial uses permitted by copyright law. For permission requests, write to the publisher, addressed "Attention: Permissions Coordinator," at the address below.

www.rwwallace.com

ISBN: [979-10-95707-19-6]

Main category—Fiction
Other category—Mystery

First Edition

14 13 12 11 10 / 10 9 8 7 6 5 4 3 2 1

Also by R.W. Wallace

Mystery

The Tolosa Mystery Series
The Red Brick Haze (free)
The Red Brick Cellars
The Red Brick Basilica

Ghost Detective Shorts
Just Desserts
Lost Friends
Family Bonds
Common Ground

Short Stories
Hidden Horrors
Critters
Gertrude and the Trojan Horse
First Impressions
Let Them Eat Cake
Out of Sight
Two's Company
Like Mother Like Daughter

Science Fiction (short stories)

The Vanguard
Quarantine
Common Enemies
Coiled Danger
Mars Meeting

Other short stories

Size Matters
Unexpected Consequences

SITTING DUCK

Bruno trusted Karen. He'd follow her anywhere.

She was a small woman but had the strength of a grown man. She had delicate features, but never enhanced them with any makeup. She had street smarts and always spoke her mind. She took charge when it was needed and told Bruno what to do when he was lost.

As she had done tonight.

Whenever Bruno hesitated over what would be the right action in any given situation, he had Karen to guide him. It was such a relief.

Still, Bruno worried *a little* about how they were to get out of their current predicament.

He chewed off the last of the nail on his thumb and started in on the index finger. He'd finished his entire left hand in the car on the way home, and the right wasn't going to give up much of a fight.

"We can't just leave her out there," he said and spit the piece of nail out of the corner of his mouth. It landed on the lip of the kitchen counter.

Karen had been about to set a wooden cutting board on the counter but paused halfway to give Bruno a level stare.

Bruno brushed the nail to the floor.

Shaking her head, Karen dropped the cutting board with a clatter and placed a knife next to it. A large plastic bag filled with something green followed.

"Don't you worry your pretty little head with that," she said. "She ain't going nowhere."

"But..." Bruno searched for words while Karen pulled the green stuff out of the bag—spinach? Maybe. Bruno only ever bought the stuff pre-cut and frozen into cubes. The only reason he recognized it was that the package sported a picture of the real deal.

He shook his head to get his mind back on the issue at hand. "What if someone finds her?"

"Why would anyone find her?" Karen efficiently sorted through the mountain of green leaves, pulling off the stems and throwing them in a pile, and lumping the leaves into a roasting pan.

"Well... She's... What if..." Bruno's hands had no more luck explaining his points than his mouth did.

"Ain't nobody going to force open the trunk of our car," Karen said as she dumped the stems in the trash under the sink. "We've lived here for three years without ever locking the bloody doors. Nobody never stole nothing, even the stuff lying about in plain sight. Why would they start now?"

She put two casseroles on the stove, one filled with water, presumably for the fresh ravioli she placed next to it, and one in which she poured half a bottle of cream. While the cream heated, she brought a disk of blue cheese out of the fridge, at least 200 grams by the looks of it. The dish was going to be less healthy than Bruno first feared.

Bruno was down to the nub on his index finger and moved on to the next one. "Maybe someone's looking for her," he said. "People tend to look for dead people."

Karen shook her head, obviously finding Bruno ridiculous. "People look for missing loved ones." She paused the cheese cutting to point her knife in the direction of the car. "Ain't nobody loving that one. In fact, I'm betting nobody will say nothing about her not showing up for work for several days—they'll be too happy to get a reprieve."

She had a point. "Still," Bruno said. "We can't just keep her in the trunk of our car. What if a dog smells her or something?"

Between setting down her knife and dumping the cheese into the now boiling cream, Karen spared a glance at Bruno. "She's wrapped up in several layers of heavy duty contractor trash bags," she said, talking slowly, as if explaining something obvious to a child. "Also, it's bloody minus ten degrees outside, like it has been for two bloody weeks. She must be frozen solid by now and won't be giving off no smells that would make dogs tick."

Bruno shuddered at the mention of trash bags. He'd been relatively okay with handling a dead body. Watching said body being cut into pieces and shoved into plastic bags? Not so much. He'd just barely managed to avoid throwing up.

In fact… "You're not using the same knife, are you?"

Karen spared a glance at the knife while she spread the cooked ravioli over the spinach. "Why? I cleaned it. Used warm water and everything." Unbothered, she poured the cheese-and-cream sauce over the pasta, placed the casseroles in the sink, and pushed the dish into the oven.

"Dinner's ready in twenty."

ೞ

Karen used the knife again while she was eating twenty minutes later. "No point in dirtying more dishes than necessary," she said when Bruno stared at the weapon.

Bruno had lost all semblance of an appetite, but when Karen pointed that blasted knife at him and said, "We have a lot to do tomorrow, eat up," he forced himself to finish his plate.

ೞ

The next morning, Bruno was startled awake by his alarm, so he must've slept a little. But it felt like he'd been awake all night, staring at the ceiling while Karen snored next to him. He always admired her *sang froid*, had been in awe of how she never let anyone mess with her or bully her around, and had done his best to emulate her in difficult situations since they started going out six months ago.

He'd thought that she could deal with anything.

He just hadn't realized that "dealing with" a colleague who was monumentally stupid, annoying, and stubborn, could mean killing her, chopping her into manageable bits, and figuring out a way of getting rid of the body.

"How are we getting rid of the body?" Bruno asked as he sipped his coffee while Karen prepared her breakfast. It was an absolute necessity for him to get some caffeine in his body, but it was out of the question to eat anything else.

Karen was using the bloody knife—again—to cut up and butter her baguette. She always carried that knife with her everywhere, but he couldn't remember seeing her actually use it before. Had he just not noticed? She was so comfortable with it.

As the thought crossed his mind, her hand slipped, and she nicked her palm.

"Would you look at that," she said. She held her hand out from her body so she wouldn't get blood on her clothes. Large drops splattered to the wooden kitchen floor.

Bruno jumped into action. "Here," he said and passed her a tissue.

"Thanks," Karen replied calmly, took it with her wounded hand, and bent down to mop up the blood on the floor.

"I…I meant for you to staunch the bleeding," Bruno said.

"Bleeding." Karen shook her head and huffed as if calling a steady stream of drops of blood "bleeding" was ridiculous.

The tissue wasn't really absorbing the blood, so she ended up rubbing the blood into the woodboards in a widening circle.

"Eh, why do I even bother." Karen straightened, dropped the bloody tissue in the trash, and picked a new one out of the dispenser, this time to use it as a bandage.

Before Bruno could figure out how to react, Karen moved on with her day as if nothing had happened. She put a large casserole on the stove, filled to the rim with water. She also started the water cooker while starting in on her baguette. From the top cupboard she eased out no less than four thermoses and lined them up on the kitchen counter.

Bruno hesitated, but couldn't stop himself from asking, "Thirsty?"

"We're going on a hike," Karen said around a full mouth. "Doin' some fishing."

"Fishing?" Bruno almost dropped his mug in surprise. "There's a dead body in the trunk of our car and you want to go fishing? Is this about having an alibi or something?"

Karen just stared at him while she chewed her bread. Bruno felt like an insect under a microscope, still alive but strapped to a cushion with a needle through his body.

When she finished chewing, she took a sip of coffee before answering Bruno. "You ain't telling nobody about our little excursion today, no, if that's what you're asking. If nobody knows when she actually disappeared, we won't need no specific alibi. We'll meet with lots of people over the next week or two, just in case."

Bruno wasn't following, but he didn't dare ask any more questions. He trusted her. He really did. She'd been nothing but a positive influence on him since they met, making him more confident and daring.

He would trust her in this.

Karen still studied him with her unnerving, unblinking green-eyed stare.

"You know she's on vacation for two weeks, right?" she finally said.

"Who, Sabrina?" He pointed in the direction of their car outside.

"Yeah," Karen said with an eye roll. "Sabrina. She kept bragging about it last night, at the party. She went on and on and on about how brilliant it was gonna be to spend two weeks in Guadeloupe or Martinique or whatever. All by herself on the beach, lickin' sun and swimming. Nobody gonna report nothing for at least two weeks. We got some leeway on the alibis."

Bruno nodded enthusiastically. "Oh, right." He thought about it some more. "But…"

Without looking at him, Karen sighed. "Just go get ready. We leave in ten minutes."

"I'll just clean the floor—"

"Don't worry about the bloody floor! Go get ready."

ও

BRUNO DID AS he was told and fifteen minutes later they were speeding down the A64 Highway in the direction of the Pyrenees. The heating was turned off completely in an attempt to conserve the car's current occupation as deep freezer. Bruno wore his aging skiing pants over a pair of worn jeans, two pairs of socks in his hiking boots, three of his warmest jumpers, and an old anorak of Karen's. His breath came out of his mouth in white puffs and he'd been sitting on his hands for the past five minutes to try to warm them up.

Karen wore her winter clothing, too, but it must be of better quality than Bruno's, because she seemed unaffected by the below-zero temperature. As she bypassed other cars and trucks, she hummed what Bruno thought was *Je veux mourir sur scène* by Dalida. The dying part was accurate enough, but Sabrina had hardly been on stage when Karen had plunged her knife into the woman's heart.

Bruno tried reasoning in his head, channeling his inner Karen. What had she meant by fishing? Was it possible to find fish that would eat the dead body? Wouldn't he have known if that existed in the area?

And what kind of alibis would they come up with? What techniques did the police have to determine when somebody died? How precise could they be? He should have watched more police procedurals on Netflix.

It was certainly a godsend that Sabrina was going on vacation for two weeks. Although…

"Won't the airline be able to tell the police that Sabrina never got on a plane? They'll know she went missing before that date. When was her flight?"

Karen stopped humming and glanced in her blind spot before switching over to the left hand lane. "Don't you trust me, Bruno? I told you, I got this."

"Of course I trust you," Bruno said. "But you talked about having an alibi for the upcoming weeks. I just don't really understand why that's necessary. Wouldn't it be more important to have it all for right now? Up until the moment her flight leaves?"

Karen took a deep breath, as if searching for strength. She let it out in a low hiss. "Her flight's on Monday morning. What you gotta remember, Bruno, is that I know what I'm doing. And you're not great under stress. So just follow my lead, don't talk to no one, and we'll be fine."

Bruno nodded and huddled into the neck of his anorak. He did trust her, and it was freeing to know that she didn't expect him to take any responsibilities. He just had to follow orders.

They exited the highway and drove past Bagnères-de-Bigorre. Another thirty minutes on an increasingly narrow road, almost a mountain trail, and they reached Chiroulet, the tiny village marking the end of this particular road.

Karen parked her car in front of the church, got out, and opened the trunk.

Bruno came rushing back, looking in all directions, searching for witnesses. "You can't just open the trunk for all and sunder to see!"

"Seriously," Karen said, her voice clipped. "You gotta take it down a notch or ten." She gestured at the open trunk. "There ain't nothing to see."

She was right, of course. There were no body parts laying around in the trunk, open for anyone to see. The body parts were stuffed into four trash bags, and on top of those bags were two large backpacks and two pairs of snowshoes.

Right. Hiking.

Karen took one of the backpacks and threw the other one to Bruno. "Shove two of the bags in here. The blue snowshoes are for you. Now let's get cracking."

With great effort and some swearing, Bruno managed to fit one of the trash bags into his backpack. While he struggled with the second bag, he glanced at the mountains behind him. The Pyrenees stretched tall and jagged to the sky, snow-covered mountain peaks giving way to frost-covered pine forest a couple of hundred meters above where they stood right now.

The sky was a blue so pure that it almost hurt to look at.

"Where are we taking the bags?" he said.

"Le Lac Bleu de Lesponne," Karen replied.

While he shoved the second trash bag into his backpack and closed the lid, Bruno glanced around again. He didn't see any lakes, blue or otherwise. "And where is this Lac Bleu?"

Karen waved a hand in the direction of the tallest peaks. "It's a two or three hour hike in that direction."

"You think I can carry this for two or three hours?" Bruno's voice cracked on the last word as he imagined being weighed down by half of the body of his deceased colleague.

"Course you can," Karen said. "That woman was tiny. She can't have weighed no more than fifty-five kilos soaking wet."

"That's still almost thirty kilos to carry for hours!"

"Nah." Karen patted the top of her backpack then swung it up on her shoulders. "There was a *lot* of blood in that bathtub. I don't know how many liters of blood we got in our bodies, but Sabrina lost a whole lot of it before we put her in the bags."

Stomach heaving at the memory of all that blood, Bruno staggered backward a couple of steps as he tried, but failed, to put his backpack on as gracefully as Karen.

She was probably right. The backpack didn't weigh thirty kilos. Still, it must be pretty close to twenty, and several hours' worth of walking in deep snow wearing snowshoes would be a rough task for someone in as mediocre shape as Bruno, even without the backpack.

"Seriously, Karen," Bruno pleaded, "I'd do anything for you, you know that. But I'm not sure I can do this."

Slamming the trunk shut, Karen slapped Bruno on the shoulder. "Sure you can. I believe in you. Besides," she added as she took off toward a mountain track at the end of the road, "at this point, you ain't really got no choice. Off we go."

Three hours later, Bruno regretted following Karen onto that track. He regretted not having gone to the police when Sabrina died. He regretted not reacting when Karen drew her knife.

He regretted being born.

His backpack weighed more than him, he was sure of it. His shoes had been soaked through for the last hour. He'd sweated through at least two layers of clothing and whenever he attempted a break to catch his breath, the wind blew right through him, making his whole body shiver with cold.

Karen was waiting for him some two hundred meters farther along the path. She seemed to have reached some sort of plateau.

In fact, she was emptying her backpack. Could they be at the lake?

Grabbing onto that little glimmer of hope with his entire being, Bruno forced his trembling legs to get moving. He followed Karen's footsteps exactly, setting his snowshoes in the yeti-like tracks hers had made. The snow was hard and crusty since there hadn't been any snowfall for well over a month, but it was still exhausting to stomp through.

Le Lac Bleu certainly carried its name well. Even covered in a thick layer of ice, it reflected the sky like a painter's perfect definition of the color blue. The Pyrenees used it to create a blue mirror image of their jagged teeth.

"See," Karen said as she arranged the four thermoses alongside the trash bags by her feet. "Told you you could do it."

Bruno didn't even have enough energy to reply. He just dropped his backpack where he stood and sat down on top of it.

The thought of sitting on Sabrina's dead body parts would have made him shudder, except he was already using all his energy to shake because of the cold wind sifting through his wet clothes.

Besides, he was too tired to care.

Karen slapped him on the back of the head. "Don't stop, idiot. You'll freeze to death. There's still work to be done."

Bruno shakily got to his feet, hissing in a deep breath when a gust of wind hit him square in the back.

"Wh—what do I need to do?" he asked.

"Bags out. Drag them out to the middle of the lake."

Bruno stared out at the large expanse of blue ice in front of him. "Out on the ice?"

Karen rolled her eyes. "Yes, out on the ice. It's on its deepest about two thirds of the way to our left." She pointed. "And halfway across to the other side. When you've brought your bags over, you can bring five rocks from the shore here. As big as you can carry."

Arms drawn around himself, Bruno stared at the trash bags as he halfheartedly bumped one of them with the tip of his boot. "We're dumping them in the lake?"

"Got it in one."

"Won't someone find her? This looks like a nice place to come for a hike in summer." The Pyrenees rose tall around them, forming an imposing and silent theater around the lake. To the north, they had an unimpeded view of the plains with Toulouse just barely visible on the horizon, if you knew where to look.

Karen put the thermoses into a smaller backpack which seemed to already contain some tools, then hefted one of the trash bags. "Le Lac Bleu is the deepest lake in the Pyrenees. Over a hundred meters where we're aiming at. We just make sure no bits float up to the surface and she won't never be found."

Bruno wasn't about to argue. He carried both his bags to the spot Karen indicated, happy for the workout to make him somewhat warm again, but unhappy about the added effort it demanded of his already exhausted body.

While he made two trips to bring the rocks Karen had asked for—ballast he supposed—Karen attacked the ice.

Bruno, who'd been looking forward to a cup of hot tea, had tears coming to his eyes when he saw her empty the last of the thermoses to melt the ice.

"You couldn't save at least a cup?" he asked, unable to keep the question in.

Karen shot him a quick glare. "Every drop saves me time with the drill. I'd have taken more if I'd had more thermoses. Stop being such a wuss."

Bruno's teeth were chattering so loud, his entire skull shook with the reverberations. "But I'm so c—cold," he whined.

"I know," Karen said.

She pulled a small drill out of her pack and set to work. The warm water had worked its charm, so it didn't take her long to cut down to the water, creating a multitude of small holes to achieve a circle about fifty centimeters across. Using a hook she'd also carried with her, she pulled the "lid" out and pushed it to the side.

"One rock per bag," she told Bruno. "No attaching on the outside. Open the bag, shove the rock in, and close it again."

Bruno tried to comply, he really did, but his fingers were unable to undo the knot on the trash bag.

"Seriously," Karen said as she hunkered down to do it for him. "You're worthless."

Bruno didn't care anymore. He just wanted to go home.

Karen made quick work of the bags, and one by one, dropped them unceremoniously into the hole. They all sank quickly, and Bruno watched them descend until they disappeared in the pure blackness below.

The lid fit right back into its original slot.

"Th—that w—will be v—v—visible," Bruno said, battling with his body to get it to cooperate.

Shrugging, Karen gathered her tools in her bag and started walking back to shore. "It'll freeze back in place. And there's snow coming over the next couple days—first snow in a month—so that'll cover it right up. Besides, it just looks like someone tried some fishing."

Bruno followed her back to their backpacks. He shouldered his, empty and blessedly light now, and followed as Karen led the way down, toward their car.

ಞ

HIKING UPHILL WITH a heavy backpack had been exhausting, but if Bruno thought the descent would be easier, he was woefully wrong.

His thighs had protested going up; they screamed in agony after thirty minutes of going down. His knees felt like they'd pop out of their joint at any moment, and he was suddenly aware of blisters having formed on his heels, making each step a trial.

He'd been hot and uncomfortable in his own sweat on the way up; he was turning into a Popsicle on the way down. His body wasn't producing enough heat and the wind just. Wouldn't. Stop. Blowing.

He couldn't feel his fingers or his toes, and his fingers were whiter than the snow he was trudging through. His thighs and ass felt like lumps of ice. His back sent shivers and panic messages to the rest of his body every time his half-frozen sweater touched his back.

With every step, Bruno told himself, *You can't stop or you'll freeze to death. One more step. You can do one more step.*

Karen trudged along ahead at a steady pace, stopping now and then to let Bruno catch up. Bruno had known she was in better shape than him but suspected the superior quality of her clothing also had something to do with her being so much better off.

She kept talking about Martinique. She'd decided that was the destination Sabrina had kept yapping about during the party.

"That's where they drink rum, right?" she mused. "Beaches and booze. That's what she said, anyway. Was going to stay at some cheap hotel and sleep her way to better accommodations. If she can do it…" She hitched her backpack higher on her back as she skipped over a small boulder.

"Hey, Bruno? Me and Sabrina could look alike, right? Same height. Face has sort of the same shape. She's hella skinnier than me, but that doesn't show on a passport photo."

The next time Bruno caught up with her, she had changed the subject, and Bruno suspected his mind was playing tricks on him.

"Where do you go to get a wig done real quick? Those shops that sell Halloween costumes?"

ღ

When Bruno finally spotted the Chiroulet church spire, his breath caught on a sob. Just a few hundred meters more, and he'd be in the car. He could remove all his clothes, put the heating on its maximum and stuff his toes on the dashboard.

Karen wouldn't like it, but Bruno had frankly had enough of Karen for today.

She was waiting for him at a spot where the trail turned into a forest track.

"Why don't you sit 'n wait here," she said, pointing at the trunk of a fallen oak. "I'll get the car and pick you up. You don't need to walk no more."

Bruno was seated on the trunk before he could even think about it. His body had accepted the invitation without checking with his brain. Then again, he was pretty sure his brain was slowing down, so maybe it wasn't such a bad idea.

"Great," Karen said and slapped Bruno on the shoulder. "See you in ten."

Despite his arched back, Bruno's sweater touched his back and he hissed in a shuddering breath.

Karen disappeared around the next bend and Bruno stayed immobile to minimize contact with his clothes.

He was so cold he wasn't even shivering anymore. He just sat there, feeling his body turning into ice at an alarming rate.

His brain decided to give one last kick: what guarantee did he have that Karen would come back for him?

His mind was about to go blank again, but he forced out a full-body shake and followed his original thought.

They hadn't been together all that long. Six months and living together for the past two weeks. Bruno had never met her family, nor any friends outside of their place of work. He didn't know anything about her past since he never asked any questions, and she never offered any information.

She knew everything about *him*, because she asked questions and he happily answered.

What if she just left him here? What would happen then?

Suddenly, he could see it. She'd find some other means of transport than their car—an Uber or hitchhiking—to get home to Toulouse for a hot meal and a long shower.

She'd go over to Sabrina's place, using the key they'd taken from her purse. Find her passport, tickets, and whatever else might be of value. She'd probably even pack a suitcase with Sabrina's things, to make it look right.

She'd figure out where to get a wig that would make her look like Sabrina.

And on Monday, she'd be on the flight for Martinique.

Would she be on the return flight? Probably not.

Which would make it look like Sabrina had disappeared in Martinique, not Toulouse.

Karen was the one who would be missing from Toulouse. Karen, whose blood was rubbed into their kitchen floor.

Whenever a woman was killed or went missing, the husband or boyfriend was always the prime suspect.

And where would Bruno be? Probably right here, frozen to death, looking like he'd just worked his ass off to get rid of his girlfriend's body.

It was tempting to just give up.

But Bruno was discovering a new source of energy, one he was wholly unfamiliar with.

Anger.

How dare she do this to him? He'd been nothing but adoring and nice to Karen, and this was how she repaid him?

He wouldn't have it.

Screaming in pain, he pushed up into a standing position. He wobbled but managed to steady himself.

The first house of the village couldn't be far. He'd made it up to the Lac Bleu and back, he could manage a couple hundred meters more.

He took the first step.

THANK YOU

Thank you for reading *Sitting Duck*. I hope you enjoyed it!

I wrote the first pages of this story for a writing class assignment, where two characters were to have a conversation while they were cooking. I had fun writing those pages, so I just ran with it and finished the story.

If you liked the story, you might want to check out some of my other books mentioned on the next page. It's mostly Mysteries, but a few short stories or other genres will pop up, too.

And don't forget that the first book of my *Tolosa Mystery* series, *The Red Brick Haze*, is available for free on my website.

R.W. Wallace
www.rwwallace.com

Also by R.W. Wallace

Mystery

The Tolosa Mystery Series
The Red Brick Haze (free)
The Red Brick Cellars

Ghost Detective Shorts (coming soon)

Just Desserts	*Common Ground*
Lost Friends	*Heritage*
Family Bonds	*Eternal Bond*
Till Death	*New Beginnings*
Family History	

Short Stories

Critters	*First Impressions*
Let Them Eat Cake	*Out of Sight*
Two's Company	*Hidden Horrors*

Gertrude and the Trojan Horse
Like Mother Like Daughter

Urban Fantasy (short stories)

Unexpected Consequences

Science Fiction (short stories)

The Vanguard

Lollapalooza Shorts

Quarantine	*Coiled Danger*
Common Enemies	*Mars Meeting*

Adventure (short stories)

Size Matters

www.ingramcontent.com/pod-product-compliance
Lightning Source LLC
LaVergne TN
LVHW041718060526
838201LV00043B/802